CHLOE *by* DESIGN

DESIGN
Destiny

BY MARGARET GUREVICH

ILLUSTRATIONS & PHOTOS BY BROOKE HAGEL

 STONE ARCH BOOKS™
a capstone imprint   www.capstonepub.com

Chloe by Design is published by Stone Arch Books
A Capstone Imprint
1710 Roe Crest Drive
North Mankato, Minnesota 56003
www.capstonepub.com

Library of Congress Cataloging-in-Publication Data
Gurevich, Margaret, author.
Design destiny / by Margaret Gurevich ; illustrated by Brooke Hagel.
pages cm. -- (Chloe by design)

Summary: As the design competition progresses, contestants are eliminated
until only three are left for the final challenge: Chloe, Nina, and Derek —
but only one can win the grand prize of an internship in New York.

ISBN 978-1-4342-9180-6 (hardcover) - ISBN 978-1-4965-0072-4 (eBook PDF)

1. Fashion design--Juvenile fiction. 2. Television game shows--Juvenile
fiction. 3. Reality television programs--Juvenile fiction. 4. Competition
(Psychology)--Juvenile fiction. 5. New York (N.Y.)--Juvenile fiction.
[1. Fashion design--Fiction. 2. Reality television programs--Fiction. 3.
Competition (Psychology)--Fiction. 4. New York (N.Y.)--Fiction.] I. Hagel,
Brooke, illustrator. II. Title.
PZ7.G98146Dd 2014
813.6--dc23
                                        2013048918

Designer: Alison Thiele
Editor: Alison Deering

Photo Credits: Kay Fraser, 71

Artistic Elements: Shutterstock

Printed in Canada.
032014   008086FRF14

Measure twice, cut once
or you won't make the cut.

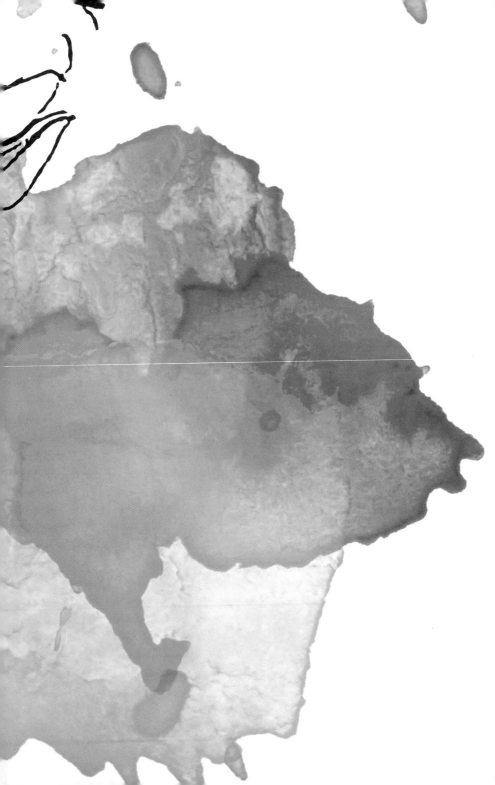

"Relax," my mom tells me as I bounce on the bed in our New York City hotel room. It's been two days since the last challenge, and I'm still pumped up from my team's win.

"I'm trying to," I tell her. "I just can't take the suspense. We're supposed to meet today, and I still haven't heard any details."

Just then, my phone beeps with a text, and I scramble to grab it. The text from the judges is short and sweet. "Lobby. Now."

When I get to the lobby, the *Teen Design Diva* judges, Jasmine, Hunter, and Missy, are already there, standing by a large, opaque screen. As usual, they're surrounded by producers and the camera crew. One by one, the remaining designers trickle in. There are only seven of us left now, and we're all wearing the same look of nervous anticipation.

"It's good to see you all again," Missy says. "I hope you all used the past two days to replenish your creativity because there are only three challenges left before we get down to the top three designers. That means the grand prize, an internship with a famous designer, is almost within reach. The next two weeks," she finishes, "will be intense."

"And because of that, we've decided that for the next few tasks, you'll be getting some help," Hunter chimes in.

At his words, my fellow designers and I exchange confused looks. *What kind of help?* I wonder. Thankfully, the judges don't keep us in suspense for long.

"Our goal in this competition is to help you become stronger designers," Jasmine says. "What better way to do that than to learn from other success stories?"

"So after careful screening of your skills and personalities," Hunter says, "we've paired you with willing mentors. Just to be clear, your mentor is not here to do your work for you. But their expertise will help you greatly."

"Especially because not too long ago, they were in your shoes," Missy adds. She points toward a nearby screen. "When the screen moves, you'll see your mentor on the other side holding a sign with your name."

With that, Jasmine waves her hand, and the screen drops. Standing behind it are contestants from past seasons of *Design Diva*. The cameras are poised to capture our reactions, but when I see who's holding my name, I'm so excited I almost forget all about the filming. It's Liesel McKay, my number-one *Design Diva* role model. I met her once before, back in California. Her son, Jake, introduced us at the final round of auditions for the show. I went to her store when I first got to New York, but she wasn't there. At least I got to see Jake, though. That made the trip worth it.

"Liesel!" I exclaim. "I mean Ms. McKay."

"Liesel, please," she says with a smile as she walks toward me. "Ms. McKay makes me feel old."

"Is this okay?" I ask. "Do the judges know we've met?"

Liesel nods. "Yep, that's why they thought I'd make the perfect mentor for you," she says. "We already know each other! Ready to head out and discuss strategy?"

"Definitely!" I say. "Where to?"

Liesel walks toward the doors leading out of the hotel lobby. "We're headed to inspiration."

* * *

"I keep a notebook with me all the time," Liesel tells me as we stroll down the crowded sidewalk . "I write down everything. You never know what might come in handy. I've woken up from dreams, jotted stuff down, and in the morning found 'banana peel' in my notebook. Then I spend all day trying to figure out what it means." She laughs.

"Do you always figure it out?" I ask.

"Not always, but it's worth writing down anyway," Liesel says. "My biggest fear is running out of ideas. It's probably the biggest fear of most designers, honestly."

I can't believe that someone as successful as Liesel McKay worries about running out of ideas. All of her clothes are so creative — and she makes jewelry and accessories on top of that. It seems like her creativity is never-ending.

"I have the opposite problem at the moment," I tell her. "The show gives us ideas. It's figuring out what to *do* with them that's hard."

Liesel nods. "Yeah, some of them are really out there. But I watched the previous challenges, and you're definitely improving. It seems you're connecting with the work more."

I nod, thinking about what Jake, Liesel's son, told me about "making a connection." "I think I have Jake to thank for that," I admit. "I came by your store a few days ago, and that's the exact advice he gave me. Does he know you're my mentor?"

Liesel laughs. "Yes. It was impossible to keep it a secret from him. The producers made him sign papers swearing his life away if he breathed a word."

"I can't wait until everyone knows everything," I tell Liesel. "I hate not being able to talk with Alex about the challenges. She's my best friend from back home. Not being able to tell her what's going on is torture!"

"I think I have something that what will put you in a better mood," Liesel says with a secretive grin. When she smiles, she has a dimple in her cheek, just like Jake.

When I spot a giant sculpture of a needle threading a button, I suddenly realize where we are — the Garment District. It's been on my list of must-sees since I first watched *Design Diva*. High-profile designers walk these streets every day. I bet Liesel knew coming here would provide the inspiration I need.

In minutes, we're standing in front of the fabric store to end all fabric stores. Liesel certainly meant it what she said about having something to put me in a better *mood*. The sign in the window says it all — Mood Designer Fabrics.

I can't believe I'm actually here. I gaze at the building, imagining shelf after shelf of amazing fabric inside. I whip out my phone, snap a photo of the store, and send it to Alex. That's not breaking the rules. After all, I could be here on my own, no matter what was happening in the competition.

"Shall we?" Liesel says. She holds the door open for me, and I follow her into the elevator.

"Mood?" the elevator operator says knowingly. Liesel nods and he pushes the button for the third floor.

Minutes later the doors whoosh open, and I'm transported to heaven. There are rows and rows of fabric in every type of material, print, and color imaginable. Mannequins wearing designs are positioned around the store, and there are buttons, accessories, and thread everywhere. It's like I'm in a design sanctuary. I don't know which direction to go first.

Liesel seems to sense how overwhelmed I am. "I could so easily go bankrupt in here," she says. "Promise me you won't let me spend more than a hundred dollars today."

"I'll try," I say. It's a good thing we're not allowed to use our own materials for challenges, or I'd be working off my debt for the rest of my life. Today, I'll just browse.

"Follow me," says Liesel. "And pay attention to what you see."

It's hard to know what Liesel has in mind, so I try to take in everything. Swatch, the adorable bulldog and unofficial store mascot I've seen on *Design Diva*, sits on the carpet. Beside him, college students sift through earring pieces. Behind them, two elderly men measure out yards of fabric. Two punk-looking guys and two women in business suits flip through bolts of plaid fabric, while a Girl Scout troop examines hair accessories.

Liesel stops. "So what do you think?"

I frown. *About what?* I think. "I'm sorry," I say, feeling like I've failed her. "I don't understand the question. What should I have been looking at?"

Liesel smiles. "Everything."

"Um . . . there was a lot to see," I say slowly.

Liesel studies me. "You mean you didn't notice the uniformity among the customers? You missed the pattern?"

Darn it! I knew this place was over my head. Should I make something up? No, I decide. *Better to just go with the truth. I don't want to embarrass myself any more than I already have.*

"No," I admit, avoiding Liesel's gaze. "I didn't."

Liesel claps her hands. "Great!"

"Excuse me?" I say, feeling like Clueless Chloe.

"There *is* no pattern," Liesel says, grinning. "That's the point. There are all sorts of people here. And you might *think* you know what they're going to like, but you'd be wrong. Thinking outside the box is what will make your designs successful. Take an idea and run with it, even if you're not sure it's what the judges want. Because you know what?"

"What?" I ask.

"Even they don't know what they want!" Liesel says with a laugh. "The lack of pattern and uniformity is what makes fashion so fun. No two designers are the same. Even if everyone uses the same materials, the end results will be unique."

I nod. Liesel's advice sounds just like what my mom told me about Nina LeFleur, my number-one rival from back home, stealing my ideas — what she does doesn't affect me. I'm my own designer. I have to remember that.

"Remember that there's more than one way to make a connection," Liesel continues. "The first step is to connect to yourself. Know your design aesthetic and go from there. But don't be afraid to let in some outside inspiration and think outside the box."

Liesel and I spend the next two hours wandering the aisles, discussing fabrics and designs. She shows me color combinations I would have never thought of, and I take notes on design techniques. By the time my phone beeps with a text about the next challenge, Liesel has spent $99.99, and I've managed to accumulate some priceless information.

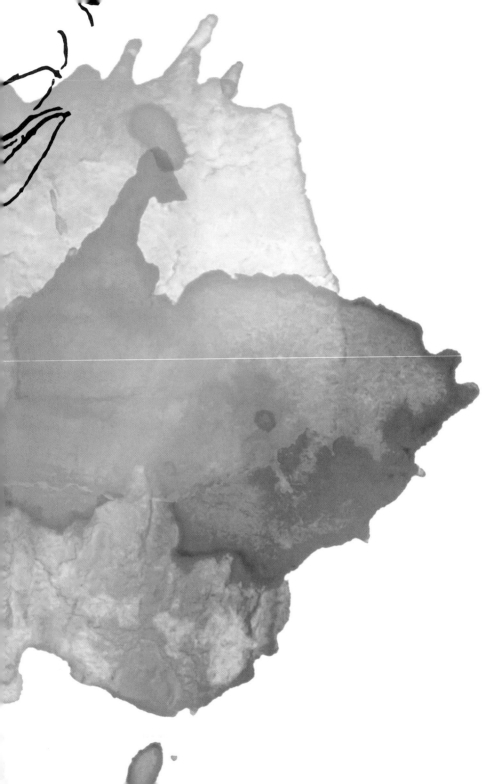

The next morning, the remaining designers are up bright and early. Our next challenge starts at 7:30 a.m. at the Sony Wonder Technology Lab, and no one wants to be late. At least this time, we won't be forced to face the judges alone. Our mentors are there beside us.

"Welcome to the Sony Wonder Technology Lab," Hunter says. "As you can see, Missy and Jasmine aren't here today. Instead, we'll be joined by two guest judges — Carmine Franklin and Jerome Grubin. You may not recognize their names, but you know their work. Carmine and Jerome both helped create the world-building games: *Choose Your Destiny and It's All Up to You.*"

No way! Those are the most amazing video games ever. They let you create a future life, from career to clothing to the entire city you live in. I always make myself a fashion designer, and I'm betting the other six contestants do the same.

"Now that we're down to seven contestants, there will be no top and bottom five," Hunter tells us. "Instead, we will have two top spots, two middle, and three bottom. And only one person will be let go this round. Make sense?"

Everyone nods, and Hunter grins. "Great. That brings me to today's good news. From here on out, there will also be a winner each challenge. For this challenge, the prize will be the opportunity to work with both Carmine and Jerome to create a line of clothing for other avatars to wear."

All around me, the other designers gasp with excitement. I'm right there with them. Imagine players throughout the world choosing my designs for their avatars!

Hunter laughs. "So now do you believe me about this challenge being fun? You'll have two hours to explore the lab with your mentor. Find an exhibit that speaks to you. When you're done, you'll have another two hours to design and create something that showcases the essence of this museum. Got it? Good. Your time starts now."

Liesel and I head for the glass elevator, which looks like something out of a science-fiction movie. We take it up to the fourth floor, and I overhear a guide giving a tour. "Everything you do here," she's saying, "creates an impact on the lab and one another."

I file that away for a possible design theme, then walk with Liesel to get our ID cards. Nothing is ordinary here. For the cards, we type our names, choose a color and music genre we like, take our picture, and record our voices. Our digital profiles will be used to help personalize our experience.

Once we have our personalized ID cards, Liesel and I move on to the Robot Zone, which lets visitors program one of six colored robots, each equipped with light and touch sensors. I choose a blue robot, Liesel chooses yellow, and we direct our robots around the circle. The sensors determine how the robots interact.

"I think our robots like each other," I say as Liesel's yellow guy follows my blue one.

"Are there enough for us?" a voice asks from behind me. I turn and see Nina and her mentor, Tanya Heartly, designer of Heart Jeans, standing behind us. Nina looks irritated, as if I've already told her she can't play.

"Sure," I say, and Nina picks a green robot. Her robot circles the ring, trying to interact with the others. When it moves closer to mine, the blue robot quickly scoots away.

I want to laugh, but Nina looks angry. "I can't control what it does," I say. "They interact on their own."

"Whatever," Nina mutters.

"You don't need them," her mentor says. "Let's go." With that, the two of them leave to check out the other exhibits.

"Don't worry about them," Liesel says, shaking her head. "She and Tanya seem to be a good fit."

"Yeah? What's Tanya like?" I ask. "Did you spend much time with her on your season?"

Liesel shrugs. "I tried to avoid her for the most part because she can be pretty cutthroat. During our season, she sabotaged some of the other designers. She never admitted it, but we knew it was her."

I push thoughts of Nina out of my head and follow Liesel to the Interactive Floor. There we stand on circles of colored light that expand and contract as we move. The more we move, the more the circles interact.

"How much time is left?" I ask Liesel.

"About an hour. You should probably think about the direction you want to take your designs," she suggests.

I've been thinking about it since we walked in. I scan the remaining exhibit summaries to find one that will mesh best with the idea that's been brewing in my head. "Let's go to the Shadow Garden and Sand Interactive," I say.

The exhibit is crowded with people. Cascading colored sand reacts to the shadows projected on the wall. I get in on the action, watching the sand accumulate based on the shapes my shadow creates. When I dance, the sand forms a line. When I move my right arm, the sand follows. The more our shapes change, the more sand accumulates. I watch someone step away from the wall, and the sand design he made falls.

I think about all the exhibits I've seen today. One robot's actions affected another's. The colored circles only stayed in place if we were all there. And the sand only worked if someone was there to engage it. In one way or another, each exhibit was influenced by the environment around it.

Interactivity, that's my inspiration. Now I just have to turn it into something wearable.

My ideas!!

SONY
TECH LAB
Sketches

SONY TECH LAB

Tiled MIRROR DRESS

Futuristic + MODERN SHAPE

REFLECTS ITS SURROUNDINGS

2nd "MIRROR" DESIGN →

SHADOW Sketches

Disco ball-esque

Reflection/ SHADOW
SHINE
SHARP
SLEEK

EXHI
VISI

EDGY TOP ↓

SHADOW GARDEN Inspired

SHEER "SHADOW" TOP

FEATHERED HEM, SHOWING AIR + Movement ↗

SONY IDEAS:
♡ SHADOWS + SHADOW GARDEN
♡ Reflection + Movement
♡ MODERN + HIGH-TECH Edge.

Floral Shadow Silho. PRINTS

People shadow print ↗

· S
· INT
· R
· S

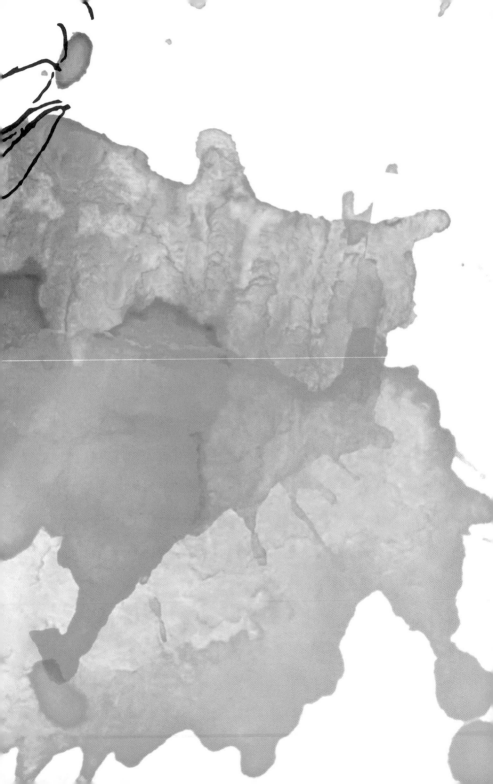

3

When our two hours of exploration are up, all the designers gather back at the entrance. Hunter leads us into a room filled with tables, sewing machines, and fabrics. Today's shelves are overflowing with different fabrics.

"Designers, you will have two full hours to complete your designs," Hunter reminds us. "Your mentors are here to oversee your designs and offer advice, but you must do all designing and garment construction on your own. Are we clear?"

All the designers and mentors nod in agreement. I'm already mentally sketching my idea and envisioning my materials so I can get started as soon as Hunter gives us the go-ahead.

"And remember," Hunter tells us, "your design should be inspired by something you saw in here today. Ready? Go!"

Right away I spot a bolt of silver crepe on a rack off to the side. I reach out and feel the soft material with my hand. This silky, flowy fabric is exactly what I need. The way it moves and flows reminds me of how the sand moved with my body in the Shadow Garden and Sand Interactive.

On a nearby rack, I spot a bolt of mirrored, metallic fabric. Jackpot! That will be the perfect accent. And even better, the contrast between the two materials — light and dark — is reminiscent of the contrast my shadow created when it was projected against the wall.

I grab the mirrored fabric, hold it up against the silver, and admire the combination. "What do you think?" I ask Liesel.

Liesel eyes the metallic material I picked. "I love the contrast," she says. "How are you planning on putting them together?"

"I'm going to use the crepe for the majority of the dress because it moves so well," I explain. "I was thinking of doing something with one shoulder and maybe adding a loose, flowy sleeve. And then I want to use the mirrored fabric at the waist to add shape and definition. It will look almost like a cut-out."

I hold the pieces up against the mannequin as I explain my vision, and Liesel nods. "The mirrored inset will help add some structure to the looser fabric, too, which I love," she says. "Seems like you have it all figured out. But how does your design fit into the challenge? What's the connection to the exhibits we saw?"

I alternate between working and talking. I have way too much measuring, cutting, and stitching to do to stop and chat for very long. "The way the material falls reminds me of the sand in the Shadow Garden," I explain. "Whenever someone walked away, it sort of cascaded to the ground. And the reflective material I'm using is there to represent my biggest takeaway — that all the exhibits we saw today were reflections of their environment."

Liesel looks impressed. "You're really on to something, Chloe," she says. "Keep it up and I might have to carry your stuff in my store after all this is over." She winks at me.

A design with Liesel? Now I know I'm definitely dreaming. But if I want that dream to come true, I'd better get to work. I start draping the silver crepe across my dress form, trying to work with the flow of the material. I don't want the dress to look sloppy, so I need the top to be fitted enough to balance out the looser, knee-length skirt I have planned for the bottom.

"One hour!" yells Hunter as lights from a nearby camera shine in my face.

Next I grab the mirrored fabric I'll be using at the waist of my dress. I hold it up against the mannequin so I can measure correctly, then get to work with the cutting. So far so good.

I finish measuring and race over to the sewing machine. Thank goodness we have access to them now. Sewing by hand would make this challenge almost impossible. I pin the mirrored material to the silver fabric and use my marking chalk to keep track of where to attach it. I'm comfortable with sewing these pieces together. The stitching reminds me of attaching the faux leather panels in some of my earlier designs.

"Thirty minutes remaining!" calls Hunter. "Thirty minutes!"

I think about what Liesel told me in Mood about there being more than one way to make a connection. I was always so worried about switching things up that I didn't focus on what I did best. It's completely possible to use similar techniques from one design to the next and still produce a fresh, new product.

I add a side zipper to my dress and carry the nearly finished garment back over to the dress form to make sure it fits. Once I'm satisfied with the tailoring, I grab a steamer to use the final few minutes to get rid of the wrinkles in the material. In earlier tasks, I might have panicked and settled for good enough, but not today. I want this design to be perfect.

"And time," says Hunter. "Hands up."

When it's time for the judging to start, I stand nervously beside my dress and wait. Hunter and the two guest judges, Carmine and Jerome, walk from design to design, finally stopping at Daphne's structural fluorescent green top and metallic skirt.

"Here's what I like," says Jerome. "Your bold color choices show you're not afraid to take risks. That's important in the design world." Daphne beams happily. Painted-on neon is so not my style, but apparently Jerome feels differently.

"The problem I have," Jerome continues, "is this silver, crinkly material you chose for the skirt. What is it exactly?"

"Mylar," says Daphne quietly.

"Like what balloons are made of?" Carmine asks, looking confused.

Daphne nods. "My theme was 'Wave of the Future.' That's what the museum represented to me." Her voice shakes. If Missy were here, she'd jump to comfort Daphne.

"Hmmm," says Jerome, checking the stitching. "Thank you, Daphne."

Luke is up next. His mannequin is wearing a silver metallic dress with sequins and studs on the shoulders.

"I see someone else was going for the look of the future, too," Hunter comments.

"That's right," says Luke. "I used metallic fabric and added to the shine with studs and sequins."

Carmine feels the pointy studs Luke used to embellish the shoulders of his dress. She smiles. "I'm not sure studded shoulder pads are my style, but your perspective is very clear. I have to commend you for that."

Luke's smile doesn't waiver. "To each his own, right?"

Hunter moves over to Derek, whose design, as usual, is flawless. "Tell us about your design, Derek."

"I was inspired by the animation exhibit here," Derek says. "Usually, what happens behind the scenes of technology is a mystery. But here, when I made my own animation, I got to see how it worked."

"So how does that play into your design?" Carmine asks.

Derek turns the skirt inside out and reveals hidden pockets. "I added these interior pockets to this high-low skirt," he explains. "They're hidden but still useful."

Carmine looks impressed. "You took the idea and ran with it." She returns the skirt to its correct side and runs her

hand down the fabric. "You can't even see where the pockets were sewn in. Your stitching and construction are flawless."

The judges move on to the next designer, Nina.

"Nina, what do we have here?" Hunter asks.

Nina squares her shoulders and gives the judges a wide smile. "I made a dress-and-headband combo, and I call it 'Silent Voices.'" She stares at the judges expectantly like they're supposed to know what she means by that.

Hunter clears his throat. "Well, uh, how about you explain how that theme works with your pieces."

Nina keeps smiling and shows off the taffeta dress she's made. "I incorporated the same material into her oversized hair bow," she says. "The material is noisy, but that's the irony. Technology may make a lot of noise, but it's, like, the uh, unrecognized parts of our world."

Huh? I think. The judges look confused too, and I spot Tanya shaking her head. Nina shoots her a confused look. I bet Tanya told Nina what to say, and she flubbed it.

"You're right, Nina. There is a lot about technology we don't know," Hunter says, trying to throw her a bone. "Thanks for sharing."

Then it's my turn. Liesel squeezes my shoulder as the judges approach. Before they can even ask me what inspired me, I blurt out, "I was inspired by the different interactive exhibits and how they reflected their environments."

Jerome laughs a little at my obvious enthusiasm, and Carmine and Hunter study the dress's construction.

"I like your choice of materials," Jerome says. "The mirrored panel at the waist is the perfect contrast to the rest of the dress in terms of both structure and material."

Carmine nods. "I agree. Can you tell us more about why you chose these two fabrics in particular?"

I take a deep breath. "As I said, I was inspired by the interactive exhibits, particularly the Shadow Garden and Sand Interactive. I chose this silver crepe because there's real movement in the material. The way it falls and waves reminds me of how the sand cascaded to the ground when someone stepped away from the sand wall. Plus the contrast between the light crepe and the darker mirrored panel reminds me of how shadows are created in the first place."

Hunter nods, and I take it as a signal to keep going. "All the exhibits we visited today were reflections of their environment and the people interacting with them," I continue. "Nothing could exist alone. No matter what, the exhibits all reflected how we interacted with them. This reflective material I used at the waist is a literal representation of that concept."

Hunter nods again. "Well put, Chloe," he says.

The judges move on to Sam's and Shane's designs, and I hear them asking Sam a lot of questions about his choice

OTHER CONTESTANTS' *Designs*

NINA'S DRESS
WITH TAFFETA & OVERSIZED HEADBAND BOW

SAM'S DRESS
WITH DRAPEY SILHOUETTE & HYPERCOLOR

SHANE'S DRESS
WITH PLEATED SKIRT

of material and stitching technique. Hunter seems to be examining his design closely, but I can't hear what exactly he's saying. Sam always seems to come out on top, though, so I bet he's not worried.

When they're finished examining the last design, the three judges move to stand in front of the row of designers. "I can see you all really took this challenge seriously," Hunter says. "Must have something to do with the great prize. Once we've finished deliberating, we'll let you know who the lucky winner is and who will be going home."

With that, the judges leave the room, and all we can do is sit and wait. Sam and Shane are deep in whispered discussion. Daphne is staring off into space, Luke looks lonely, and Nina looks annoyed. Only Derek appears relaxed, leaning back with his hands behind his head.

After about thirty minutes, the judges reappear. Everyone immediately perks back up and pays attention.

"Let's start with our favorite designs of the day," Carmine says. "Chloe and Derek, you both impressed us with your thematic application and use of fabric. We also like how you both expanded your thinking in terms of what this challenge required."

Derek and I exchange happy grins. I'm so excited and relieved, I feel like I could burst. But the judges aren't finished quite yet.

"Now on to the not-so-good news," Jerome says. "While we did like everyone's attempt to convey a message through his or her designs, it seems like a few of you lost something in the execution. Daphne, your colors were daring, but we can't get on board with wearing Mylar. It just didn't work."

Daphne nods, but she looks like she might cry. I think of how put together she was during the team challenge at the hardware store and feel bad for her.

"Luke," Carmine says, "while I really admire how you stuck to your guns in terms of your very modern vision, I can't see anyone off the runway wearing studded shoulder pads. I'm sorry."

Hunter speaks up next. "The last person joining the bottom three today is Nina. You may have had an interesting design, but we didn't understand your concept. And unfortunately, I don't think you did either."

Nina looks up in horror. She clearly wasn't expecting to be in the bottom today.

"Sam and Shane, you're both safe for today," says Hunter. "Unfortunately, one of our bottom three will be eliminated today. Nina, although your point of view was confusing, we were able to see beyond that to what the design could be. Daphne, while we didn't like the Mylar, we liked the choice of color. Luke, I'm sorry but there were too many things that did not work for us with your piece. It just wasn't wearable, and there was no clear connection to the challenge. You'll be leaving us today."

Surprisingly, Luke takes the elimination well. "Thank you all for this opportunity," he says. "It's been a great experience. I promise you'll see me again."

"I have no doubt about that," Hunter agrees. "In fact, I look forward to it."

"Shall we end this with some good news?" Carmine asks excitedly.

"What would that be?" Jerome teases. "Oh, yes, the big winner." He pauses for effect, and my hearts pounds with anticipation. "Derek and Chloe, we really enjoyed both of your designs. However, one of them really stood out. Chloe, both your theme and execution captured the essence of this task. Congratulations! Your designs will be featured in video games worldwide!"

I can't believe it! Did he really just say my name? I think. I must not be imagining things, because in seconds Liesel is hugging me. The rest of the contestants congratulate me too. Everyone except for Nina.

I catch her looking at me and can't help but think that if looks could kill, I'd be in serious trouble.

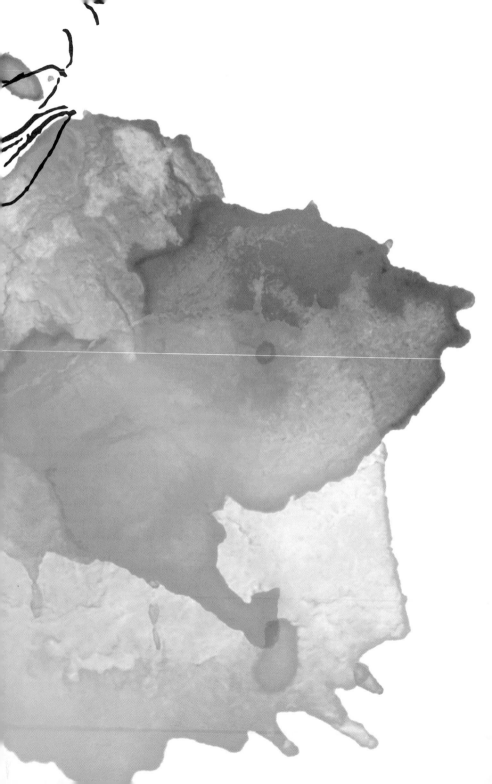

The next morning, loud shouting wakes me up from a deep sleep. I jump out of bed and run to my phone, worried I've missed a message about a new challenge.

"What time is it?" my mom asks groggily.

I look at the time on my phone. "Six a.m.," I tell her. No text from Hunter, thank goodness. But the shouting is getting louder. I open the door a crack and see Sam and Shane standing in the hallway. Both of them look devastated.

"How could you do this?" Shane shouts at his twin.

"I don't know, I panicked!" Sam yells. "I wanted to win."

"But you were doing fine," Shane says. "Now they're going to think I'm a cheater too."

"It was just some thread and a piece of fabric. It's not a big deal," Sam insists.

What thread? What fabric? I think. My groggy six a.m. brain is not putting the clues together fast enough.

"It *is* a big deal," Shane insists. "We can't use any of our own materials. You know that! Did you think the judges wouldn't notice?"

Suddenly what they're talking about makes sense. Sam must have somehow brought his own materials to the challenge yesterday. Hunter's excessive questioning about Sam's stitching and choice of material makes sense now too. He must have known something was up when the material wasn't one he recognized.

"I'm sorry," Sam says. "I'm really sorry."

"Well, sorry isn't going to cut it since you've been disqualified," Shane says. "We were going to do this together. And you ruined it."

I close the door. I'm too awake to go back to sleep. "It sounds like Sam was eliminated," I tell my mom. "He cheated."

Mom shakes her head. "Pressure gets to people," she says.

I nod but don't say anything. With Sam gone we're down to five designers, but this is not how I thought the next elimination would go.

* * *

An hour later, a producer tells me I need to meet in the lobby. The judges and the other designers are already there when I arrive.

"I'm sure by now you've heard about what happened," Missy says. "Because of that, Sam will no longer be with us."

I glance over at Shane to see how he's holding up without his twin here. It's hard to tell, though. The whole time Missy speaks, Shane stares at the floor.

"Unfortunately, Sam's disqualification has forced us to alter our elimination schedule," Hunter adds. "The bad news is there's now only one challenge left before we're down to the final three. But the good news is we'll be giving you the rest of the week off so we can regroup and adjust the schedule."

"In light of recent events, we decided it was better to give you more time in the final task," Jasmine says. "We'll have another challenge next week, after which two designers will be eliminated. The remaining three will move on to the final challenge and compete for the grand prize — an internship with a world-class designer. For the final challenge, you will be permitted to use one of your own items. We'll air the results live the following week."

Around me, the remaining designers look worried. I don't blame them. There are only five of us left now — me, Nina, Daphne, Derek, and Shane — and this is a lot of information to take in at once. Instead of two more challenges to prove ourselves, we only have one. The judges sounded like they wanted to take some of the pressure off, but all this has done is add more.

I try to remember Liesel's advice about staying positive and what Jake said about making a connection with the tasks. I've made it this far, I think. *What's one more challenge?* I look at the camera guys and give them what I hope looks like a winning smile.

Take that, pressure.

* * *

That night I dream of dresses. They come out of closets and drawers, one by one. I'm trapped in a sea of pastels, sequins, and lace as the dresses march in a parade. Some have tacky sashes, others V-necks and open backs. They lead me to a room packed with party dresses.

My sketchpad appears, and I make notes about the dresses, but suddenly Jasmine whisks it out of my hand. "The task starts now!" she says.

"Keep up the pace!" Hunter yells.

Out of nowhere, Missy calls time and rings a bell.

I jolt awake, still hearing the bell. I try to clear my head, but the bell rings and rings. Suddenly I realize where the noise is coming from — my phone. I reach for it, groggy and confused, and read the text. I have to be in the lobby in one hour to start the next challenge.

With a groan, I climb out of bed and get ready. There's no time to waste. When I get downstairs, it's like my dress dream has come to life. In the lobby, I see rack after rack of party dresses and fancy suits. But they're not fabulous by any means — they're hideous. Most of them are styles I've only seen in ancient fashion magazines or eighties movies.

"Welcome to the next challenge," Jasmine says. "As you know, today's task will determine who makes it to the final three. Because this assignment is a bit more challenging, you'll be allowed to consult with your mentors. And you'll have all day — a total of six hours — to complete your designs."

"To make things even more exciting," Jasmine continues, "I'd like to introduce our guest judge." She turns to face a nearby door, and a short, redheaded woman steps out. "Please welcome Mallory Kane, the creator of TooDressy. com. For those of you not familiar with the site, it's a rental-clothing business. The winner of this challenge will not only have his or her design added to the site — it will also be showcased as the formal piece of the month."

Holy cow! My best friend, Alex, and I are obsessed with that site. They have the most amazing designer pieces at, like, a fraction of the cost. To have my design be one of the choices? That would be unbelievable.

Missy seems to sense our excitement. "There are definitely perks to this challenge, but it won't be easy," she says. "Take some time to examine the garments in front of you. Think about what you like and what you don't."

The rest of the designers and I immediately make a beeline for the rack of dresses. Some are smooth and velvety while others are made of satin, silk, taffeta, and spandex.

After a few minutes, Hunter calls us back from the racks. "I hope you had some time to think of a vision for your design," he begins, smiling slyly. "Each of these ensembles has the potential to become something beautiful . . . if you go on what you see, that is."

What else would I go on? I think. *Ugh. I hate it when the judges are cryptic.* I glance at over at Nina, Derek, Shane, and Daphne, but they look confused too.

"For this challenge," Jasmine says, "you will have to remake one of the pieces on the rack into something that would be wearable and fashionable by today's standards."

I can see everyone relax. That's exactly what I was thinking. But then Jasmine, Hunter, and Missy walk up to the racks and start turning everything inside out.

"The hard part," says Missy, "is that you will have to transform the dress or suit as seen from the inside out."

I put my head in my hands. Suddenly an entire day of designing and sewing doesn't seem like enough time at all. *What am I going to do with the seams? How will I get the fabric to look how I want?* I think, feeling panicky. Suddenly my dreams of making it to the top three seem farther away than ever.

6

For the first time, when the judges start the clock, the usual scramble for fabric and materials doesn't happen. No one races to the racks. In fact, no one moves. We all just stare at the clothes in front of us, not sure how to begin.

Does it even matter which dress I pick anymore? I think. The concept is so far beyond the fabric and style.

"What are you thinking?" Liesel asks, moving closer.

"That this is impossible," I mutter. I notice a cameraman moving closer and avert my gaze. The last thing I need is for my self-doubt to be broadcast on national television.

Liesel looks at her watch. "I'll give you five minutes of self-defeatist thoughts and then you have to plan. Deal?"

I smile. "Deal." Maybe that's all I need, I think. To flush out the bad thoughts and then get to work.

But somehow knowing I have permission to wallow makes it harder to do so. My mind starts drifting to the dresses and what I can do to transform them into something wearable. Do I want short or long? Crinkly or not? Tight or loose?

Liesel hasn't called time on my wallowing, but I'm over it. I decide to go for an in-between option and create an asymmetrical hemline. I head back to the rack of dresses and settle on a long one with puffy sleeves and a gold sash. It is about three sizes too big, but the bright emerald green color is so striking I can't resist. Plus there are minimal seams to deal with, so I grab my sketchpad and start brainstorming.

Liesel peers over my shoulder at my sketches and nods approvingly. "See, I knew you could do it. That looks great. It's a really modern take on that dress."

Suddenly Hunter appears with a camera crew in tow. "Can you talk us through your vision?" he asks.

"Sure," I say, trying to measure, talk to him, and ignore the cameras at the same time. I make marks by the bust, then put down my fabric pen. Turns out talking and measuring looks a lot easier on television than it is in reality. "My idea is to cut strips from the gold sash and use them to cover the seams." From the corner of my eye, I see Nina stop what she's doing to listen in. "I have some cool ideas for the hem and sleeves, too, but I'd like to keep those a surprise."

Hunter nods. "A little mystery is always good. I look forward to seeing what you come up with."

Nina frowns but puts on a happy face as soon as Hunter and the camera crew move in her direction. I don't bother

trying to eavesdrop on what she's saying — I already have my design plan in place. Hearing her plans will just psych me out.

I slip the dress over the top of my dress form and start pinning the waist and bust to take it in. I work along the existing side seams and then get to work measuring where the new hem will be. I'll have to take off quite a bit of length to make the dress wearable, but the new hemline will be a modern twist on the dress, and the volume will help balance the tight waistline I'm envisioning.

Once I've cut off the bottom of the dress, as well as the puffy sleeves, I head over to the sewing machine and get to work taking the dress in. Soon I lose myself in the rhythmic hum of the sewing machine. I take my time, making sure my sewing is clean and precise. I don't need something like that tripping me up at this stage in the competition.

Once the dress is a more manageable size, I slip it back over my dress form. I still need to add a hidden side zipper, but I'll do that once I've added the fabric strips to define the waist.

Grabbing the gold sash that went with the original dress, I measure out strips of fabric several inches wide, making sure they're long enough to wrap around the natural waist of my dress. When I have the strips ready, I brush hair out of my face and step back to get a better look at what I have so far.

"Nice work," Liesel says encouragingly. "Want to break for lunch?"

I look at my watch and am surprised to see I've been at it for three hours. I stretch my hands behind my back and shake out my legs, only now noticing how cramped they are from crouching. "In another hour?" I suggest. "I want to get the metallic strips started before I take a break."

Liesel smiles, and I can tell she's proud of me. "You haven't even asked for my help!" she says.

"There's still time," I say. For now, I'm on a roll.

* * *

The rest of the time flies by. I've crisscrossed the gold strips at the natural waist of the dress, and they're the perfect accent against the gorgeous emerald material on the rest of the dress. I've sewn the strips on the bias to make them more flattering. Now they emphasize the waist perfectly and help disguise the exposed seams.

I've also eliminated the poufy sleeves of the dress, and altered the neckline. Nothing too severe — just an elegant boatneck. The higher neckline helps to balance out the newly shortened, asymmetrical hem. The overall effect changes the dress from an eighties monstrosity into a sleek gown.

But with only an hour left on the clock, my nerves start to set in. I still need to make some last-minute tweaks, like adding the hidden zipper to the side and fixing the hemline. It looks a little crooked right now, and I know that won't fly with the judges.

"What can I do to help?" Liesel asks.

"Sew for me?" I say hopefully. But I know that's the one thing Liesel can't do. Advise? Yes. Explain? Sure. Do my project for me? A big fat no. "Just kidding," I say. "What do you think it needs?"

"I think you need to take the hem out and redo it over here," Liesel says, voicing exactly what I was thinking.

"The whole thing?" I say. I immediately feel panicky. "How am I going to finish everything if I have to redo the hem?"

"You're not undoing the entire thing," Liesel says. "It'll only require minimal sewing to fix it. Trust me."

I do. It's why she's gotten this far. I reach for the seam ripper that was in my basket, but it's not there. "Where'd my seam ripper go?" I ask. "It was just here."

Liesel rummages through my scraps. "Are you sure?"

"Yes." I crouch down but don't see it anywhere.

"Forget it," says Liesel. "Get another one."

"But it was just here," I insist.

Liesel ignores me and grabs another seam ripper. I push the missing seam ripper out of my head as I undo the stitching. Lining the hem up carefully to make sure it's even and straight this time, I sew it back into place. "Done!"

Just then, Nina turns toward me, and I notice a second seam ripper at her feet. "Why do you have two?" I ask.

"Two what?" Nina replies innocently.

"Seam rippers." I look at the handles. Mine definitely had a blue handle, just like the extra one by Nina's feet.

Nina shrugs as the camera crew, sensing some growing tension, surrounds us. "I don't know," she says. "It must have rolled over here."

"Yeah, from my basket!" I can't keep my voice down.

"Don't blame me if you can't keep track of your stuff, Chloe," Nina snaps, turning away.

"Can't keep track of my—" I want to lunge at her.

"Forget about it, Chloe," says Liesel, gently tugging on my arm. "You don't have much time left. Focus on your design."

I know Liesel is right, but it's hard to focus when I'm so frustrated. And worst of all, the cameras are right there recording everything. It's going to look like I totally lost my cool — I can only hope they don't edit it to make me look too crazy.

"Santa Cruz friendship torn apart by seam ripper!" I imagine the *Teen Design Diva* commercials saying. Not that there ever was a friendship.

With a final sigh, I turn away from the cameras to put the finishing touches on my dress. I refuse to let Nina's underhanded tactics take this away from me.

7

When the judges call time, I'm ready. The other contestants and I take our spots next to our mannequins for the judging process, and I try focus on how pretty my dress turned out instead of worrying about my earlier Nina-related freak-out.

I glance over at Derek and Shane. It looks like they both opted to create menswear-inspired designs. Menswear isn't exactly my strong suit, but I'm definitely impressed. It's a totally different take on the challenge. I almost wish one of their designs could be chosen in addition to one of the dresses Nina, Daphne, and I created.

The judges begin their short walk around our creations. For a several minutes, no one says anything. Then Mallory Kane suddenly claps her hands. "Bravo!" she shouts. "I have to confess something. When I agreed to be a part of this show, I was pretty nervous about what that would mean. I've seen *Design Diva*, and some of the visions are . . . well, let's just say different from mine. I was a little bit worried about what I would do if I had to choose from a group of totally out-there designs."

Well, this is a great pep talk, I think. *Is she going to tell us how terrible she finds all our designs?*

Then Mallory smiles. "But you've all surprised me." she continues. "There's not just one design I'd be happy to display on my site — I'd love to see all of your work displayed." She frowns. "That's what makes judging so difficult."

Mallory walks around each design for the second time. When she's done pacing, she claps her hands again. "That's it!" she yells. "I've got the solution!"

Jasmine, Missy, and Hunter look alarmed. Whatever is coming was clearly not scripted. "Maybe we should talk about—" Hunter starts to say.

But Mallory doesn't let him finish. "My site, my rules," she interrupts. "I've decided that instead of just one contestant's design being showcased, I want to display two. One menswear-inspired item and one dress."

The judges quickly glance at the cameras, and their plastic smiles immediately return. "Lovely idea!" Missy says.

"What a treat for everyone!" Jasmine agrees through clenched teeth.

Derek and Shane grin at each other. Mallory's decision to change the rules must mean she likes at least one of their designs enough to keep it in the running.

"Let's start by discussing what we like about each design," Hunter says, sounding rushed.

He probably wants to get started before Mallory tries to change anything else, I think.

"Great idea," Missy says. "Nina, let's start with you. I like how you utilized satin to create a mermaid-style dress. The flared lower half really shows your command of sewing skills."

My body tenses. Nina used satin? That has to give her points with the judges since it's pretty challenging to work with.

"Thank you," Nina says. Her smile looks a little smug to me, and I have to resist the urge to roll my eyes. "I was really inspired by old Hollywood glamour."

"I like the mermaid style, too," says Jasmine. "And using satin is a bold choice." She pauses to examine the stitching of the satin and nods. "However, I can see you had some trouble with it here, here, and here."

Nina's face reddens, and she doesn't say anything.

"Overall, though, fine work," Hunter says. "You can barely tell this dress has been turned inside out."

"Thanks," Nina mumbles. She looks over at her mentor and then looks away again. Tanya clearly looks irritated, but it's impossible to tell if her frustration is directed toward the judges or Nina.

Daphne is up next. "I chose a white dress," she explains, "and dyed it to create an ombré effect. I also altered the back of the dress a bit. It was a scoop neck before, so I made it just a little bit deeper and more dramatic."

"I love this color!" Mallory gushes. "You've done such a fantastic job with the dyeing."

"I agree," says Hunter. "The color is spot on. And I love the fabric, but it seems like that's really all you did. I'd have liked to see more complexity in the design itself. It's a bit too basic for my tastes. There's no real risk there."

Daphne's face falls as the judges move on to the boys. Shane chose to go with a less-traditional suit style with pants that fall just below the knees. Derek's suit pants fall past the ankles. He also made a vest from the excess fabric, adding gold buttons to the front and creating a vertical striped design with gold thread.

"The tailoring on both of these suits is very impressive," Mallory says. "I wish we could use all of these."

"I agree with you on the tailoring," Jasmine interrupts, "but, Shane, these cropped pants are just oddly proportioned. The length of the pants isn't flattering with the blazer, and they don't really work with the overall suit design."

Shane frowns but doesn't say anything as the judges move in my direction.

"My favorite aspect of this dress," says Mallory, jumping right in, "is the asymmetrical hem. It adds just the right amount of interest to the dress."

I hardly have time to enjoy the compliment before Jasmine jumps in. "My concern is whether or not this style

OTHER CONTESTANTS' *Designs*

SHANE'S SUIT
CROPPED PANTS WITH JACKET

DEREK'S SUIT
MENSWEAR INSPIRED

will withstand the test of time," she says. "It's stylish now, but the mark of a lasting design is something that can be worn for more than a month. This is awfully trendy."

I notice Nina winking at Tanya, and I clench my fists in irritation.

"Still," says Missy, "I love the bold color. It's just stunning. And the bands of contrasting fabric around the middle are beautiful. The fabric strips are very slimming, and I adore the metallic accents. You can't tell this dress was inside out."

Jasmine glares at Missy. *What's the problem?* I wonder. Maybe it makes for bad television if they leave us feeling confident about our design. Have keep the audience — and us — guessing, I suppose.

"As Mallory said, everyone's designs today were impressive. It's clear you've all come a long way since this competition started," Hunter says. "And even though we'd like to keep you all, two designers will be going home today. When we come back, we'll reveal who will be advancing to the top three."

With that, the judges disappear. Everyone seems nervous. Daphne is looking at the ground, and I see Nina biting her fingernails. Even if she did steal my seam ripper, there's something about her hunched posture and nervous biting that make me feel sorry for her. Shane looks to the judging room, then back to his design. Even though I like his suit, he hasn't seemed the same since his brother was sent home.

I don't see Derek, but suddenly I feel a tap on my shoulder, and he's standing right behind me. "I really liked your dress," he says.

"Thanks," I say, feeling flattered. "I've liked all your designs from the start. The stuff you came up with for the rodeo challenge back in Salinas was awesome!"

Derek blushes. Sensing a moment he might need to capture, one of the cameramen gets closer. Derek rolls his eyes. "That's right, folks," he says to the cameras. "We're forming an alliance. Or are we?" He wiggles his eyebrows, and I laugh. The cameraman moves on to Shane.

"I guess we don't provide enough drama," I say.

Derek rolls his eyes again. "Fine by me," he says. "I've been trying to lie low and avoid that."

Before I can reply, the judges reappear.

"We've come to our decision," Jasmine announces. "While we agree each of the designs is special, we can only choose three to move on to the final round."

"I want to emphasize, however," Missy jumps in, as Jasmine rolls her eyes, "that we are all so impressed with how far you've come. Don't let tonight's elimination detract from everything you've accomplished."

"While all five of you did great work, two of your designs really stood out," Mallory says. "They are not only stylish, but I can see them being popular for years to come."

My heart sinks. Jasmine made it more than clear that she didn't think my dress would withstand the test of time. Mallory's statement seems like foreshadowing — even if I make it to the top three, my dress won't be featured on her site.

"Derek," Mallory says, "your command of fabric, stitching, and color makes your feminine suit a welcome addition to any wardrobe."

Derek takes a deep breath. There always seems to be a *but* following the judges' compliments — but not this time.

"Congratulations!" Mallory exclaims. "Your suit is the top menswear-inspired pick for my site!"

"Daphne, Shane, Nina, and Chloe," Hunter says, taking over, "only two of you will continue on in the competition after today. Nina, your mermaid dress was an interesting silhouette, and we were impressed by your choice of fabrics. You're safe."

I see Nina breathe a sigh of relief. From the sidelines, Tanya gives her a proud smile and a thumbs-up.

"We have one spot left in our final three," Jasmine says. "Chloe, I had questioned whether your dress would still be something teens would want to wear in the future."

Instinctively, I look at the camera. "Yes," I say. The knot in my stomach gets tighter.

"I agree with Mallory that the design will appeal for many seasons," says Jasmine. "Sorry to keep you hanging like that."

It takes me a minute to make sense of what Jasmine said. "You mean I'm safe?" I ask. I can hardly believe it. I made it to the final three!

"You're more than safe," Mallory says. "You're also our other winner. Your dress will be featured on my website. Congratulations!"

I gasp. This is too good to be true. "Thank you," I manage to say.

"Unfortunately, Daphne and Shane, that means you'll both be leaving us today," Jasmine says. "We've enjoyed your designs throughout the competition, but this round they weren't where they needed to be move on. We wish you both the best."

Shane and Daphne take the elimination better than expected, hugging everyone goodbye before leaving the room. Then there are three designers left — Nina, Derek, and me.

Derek hugs me, but Nina hangs back until Tanya whispers something in her ear. Then, she gingerly puts her arms around me and offers a forced smile for the cameras. I close my eyes, and this time the dresses of my nightmare are gone. All I see now is row after row of my emerald dress.

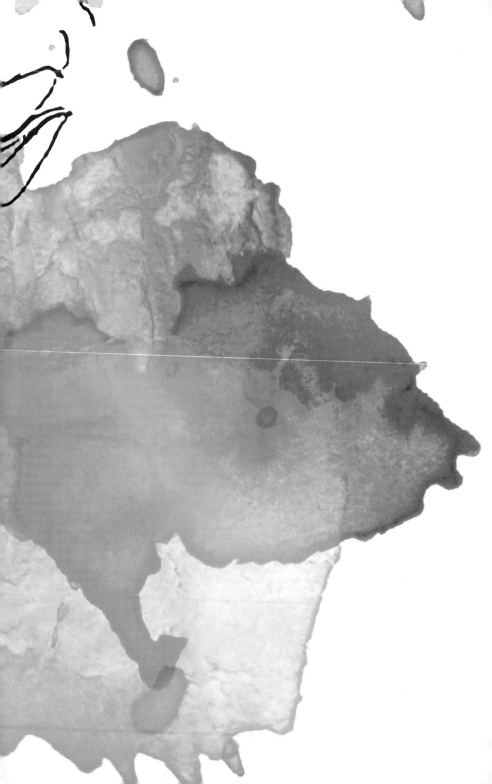

8

The night before the final challenge, I try to focus on relaxing. The internship is almost in my hands, and I don't want to freak myself out. I sprawl on the hotel bed and flip through the channels until I come across the most recent episode of *Teen Design Diva*. It's the dress challenge. They're breaking it up into two parts, with the results show airing at the end of the week.

I watch as the commercials tease what will happen in tonight's episode. They show me on my hands and knees looking for the seam ripper. Then they show me yelling at Nina and the screen freezes on my angry face. Just as the voiceover says, "Has the pressure finally gotten to be too much for one of the designers?" my phone rings.

"What the heck?" Alex says before I even say hello.

"It wasn't my fault," I tell her. "You'll see."

"Duh," Alex says. "I'm your best friend. I know that. What did Nina do?"

"I don't know for sure if she did anything," I say. "I just have my suspicions. Let's watch. You'll find out when I do."

The show does a montage of all the contestants before launching into the instructions for the challenge. There's my relieved face when we're told about the extra time and the help from our mentors. The camera stays on me as we're told about the inside-out twist, and I frown with worry. My nervous face is the last thing viewers see before the commercial break.

"I think they're trying to show your descent into madness," Alex says with a laugh.

When the show returns, they've switched gears. The cameras zoom in on Shane and Daphne, both hard at work. Hunter says something to Shane that we can't hear, and Shane nods. Then the show cuts to a confessional of Shane.

"I'm kind of done," Shane says. "Without Sam here . . . I don't know. That really got to me. I'm doing my best, but honestly I'll be fine if I go home."

"No!" Alex shouts in my ear. "Tell me he doesn't get eliminated."

"You know I can't tell you that," I say. "You have to watch to find out."

Alex grumbles, and the cameras move over to Nina, who is deep in discussion with her mentor. "I'm doing the best I can!" Nina snaps at Tanya over the top of her sewing machine.

I have to admit, Nina does seem to be working hard. Her fingers are moving quickly, and unlike mine, her basket and scraps are well organized. Hunter walks over to discuss the design she's working on, but before he can say anything, Nina shakes her head. "I'm sorry. I'm just too swamped to talk."

I can practically hear Alex rolling her eyes through the phone. "I can't believe her nerve. All hail, Queen Nina," she mutters.

The camera pans back to me. My back is to my basket as I sew the fabric strips around the waist of my dress. That's when I see it. Nina stealthily walks over to my basket and takes the seam ripper.

"Oh, no she didn't!" Alex yells. "Why is she taking your stuff?"

I'm too busy watching to answer her. I suspected this, and seeing it actually take place makes me angry all over again. The camera pans back to Tanya, who gives Nina a quick high-five. It stays on the pair, and I turn up the volume.

"That's how to do it," Tanya says under her breath. "If you really want to win, you have to be willing to do anything."

Nina is back at her machine and grinning. "I do want it," she says. "I gave her this hideous necklace while we were back home, too, and told her that's what the judges are looking for."

"Nice," Tanya says "Maybe she'll use it in the finale."

"That jerk!" Alex says. "If you're in the finale, you should use that necklace. You can make anything look amazing."

I stare at the screen, not saying anything. Even though I suspected Nina wasn't playing fair, seeing proof of it stinks. Her elbowing me in the side early on in the competition clearly wasn't an accident. Neither was my seam ripper going missing. And now the necklace.

I don't want to watch the rest of the show. I already know I freaked out on her. "I'll talk to you tomorrow, Alex," I say. "Keep watching. It gets good."

I hang up, suddenly exhausted. I know Nina wants to win, but so do I. It's like elementary school all over again. The only difference is me. When I was a kid, I would've cowered and let her win.

Not this time, I think determinedly. *I'll do exactly what Alex said. Not only will I find a way to use that ugly necklace, I'll win with it.*

9

The final challenge is held in a huge conference room in the hotel. Today, it's relatively empty — just us, the judges, the producers, and the camera crew. On Monday, it will be packed for the live finale.

"Designers," Missy says, "welcome to the final challenge! As we mentioned earlier on in the competition, for this challenge, you'll each have the option of using one item from home. Do you all have yours?"

I pat my pocket with the necklace Nina gave me back in California. That feels so long ago at this point.

Missy continues. "It's been a long road, and for one of you, the journey will continue. As you know, the prize for this winning this challenge, and the first season of *Teen Design Diva*, is an amazing fashion internship."

My heart is beating quickly, and I feel my blood pumping. The internship is almost within reach. I can't believe how far I've come since the first challenge. But I still have one final challenge to go, and the competition is incredibly stiff. Derek is a great designer. So is Nina — as much it pains me to admit it.

"For your final task," Jasmine says, taking over, "you will be required to create an outfit that can do double duty. It must be something that could be worn in the office as well as for any evening events one might be required to attend in the evening."

"You will have until five p.m. Friday night to complete this challenge," Missy tells us. "That's almost two and a half days — and more time than you've had for any other challenge — so we expect to see your best work. Your time starts now!"

I take a deep breath and focus on the challenge at hand. With so many hours to complete a task, I know I'll need a design that's extra special. I think of office wear that's inspired me in the past, and the perfect idea forms in my mind — a sheath dress with slim pencil skirt. It'll be perfect for the workplace during the day, especially if I add a removable collar.

To transform it into something that could be worn to an after-work event, I'll add a peplum ruffle at the waist that can be zipped on or off. With the peplum on and the collar off, it'll be a chic party dress. I'll use a rayon-nylon-spandex

Versatile:
Work to Gala

REMOVABLE
DESIGN IDEAS:
ZIPPER ATTACHMENTS
• PEPLUM RUFFLE

TOOLS OF THE TRADE

INTERNSHIP
DEVELOPMENT
Sketches

• Thread
• Fabric
• Accents
• Snaps
• Zippers

blend for the dress and silk cotton shirting for the collar and peplum.

It'll be a lot of work, but I need something big. At this point in the competition, it's go big or go home. And going home was never part of my plan.

* * *

"Chloe, can you talk us through your design so far?" Hunter says later that afternoon. He motions for the cameras to come closer.

I sigh. I may have gotten used to having the cameras around while I work, but that doesn't necessarily mean I like them. "I'm creating a sheath dress with a natural waist for the office," I explain. "The definition at the waist and fitted skirt will make it office appropriate, and I have some removable accents to help transform the dress depending on where it'll be worn." I try to sew while talking but give up.

Hunter nods approvingly, and the cameraman zooms in on my sketchpad. "Sounds like you have a lot of work ahead of you," Hunter says.

I smile a little nervously. "I definitely do, so if you don't mind . . ." I trail off.

Hunter laughs and motions for the cameras to follow him to Nina's station. "I can take a hint. Best of luck, Chloe."

Once he leaves, I finish marking the pattern on my fabric. I've opted for basic black for my sheath dress. Some people might think it's too boring, but to me, it screams simple and chic. You can't go wrong with the basics. The black-and-white combo will look elegant and modern, like a feminine tuxedo. Best of all, I'm staying true to my style aesthetic. I might get brave and branch out with color on occasion, but for a big challenge like this, I'm sticking with what I know.

Once I have my pattern set, I grab my fabric and head over to my sewing machine to start sewing.

"Use this," says Derek, suddenly beside me, tissue paper in hand. "If you put it under the fabric, it will keep it in place while you sew."

I have to admit, I'm surprised by the kind gesture. "Helping the competition?" I say with a laugh. "Viewers will love that."

Derek shakes his head. "I don't care about that. If I beat you, I want it to be the best you. Otherwise, how will I know where I stand?"

Even when he's not designing and sewing, Derek still impresses me. If I'm being totally honest, I don't see myself doing the same for Nina. "Thanks," I say gratefully. Out of the corner of my eye, I see Nina's shocked face. Clearly, she wouldn't do the same for me either.

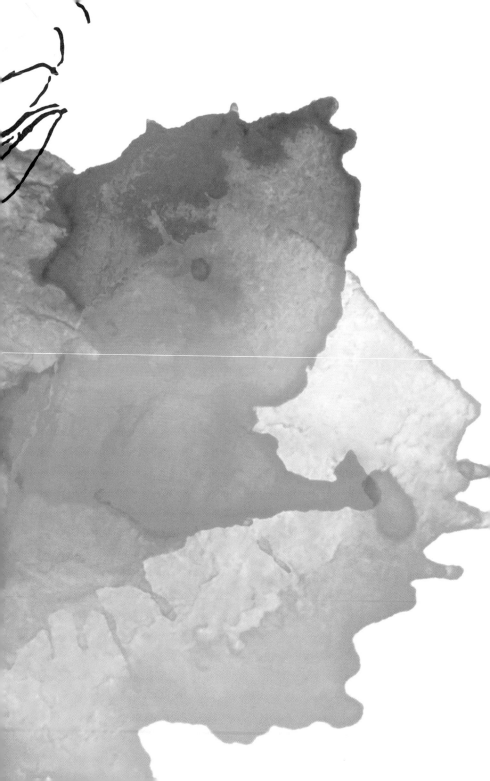

As the day continues, I only take a few small breaks. Some water here, a sandwich there, and it's back to the machine. I don't have any time to waste if I want to finish my dress in time.

It's past nine when Jasmine walks over to my station to check out what I've accomplished so far. "This is an interesting choice of material," she says. From her tone of voice it's impossible to tell if she means interesting in a good way or a bad way.

But at this point, does it really matter? I think. *I don't have time to redo it either way.*

Jasmine continues inspecting my work so far, focusing on the seams, while I watch nervously. I've tapered the waist of my dress and added darts to make it slimming. But Jasmine is notoriously hard to impress, and her facial expression gives nothing away.

"It looks like you've made some good improvements from the shift dress we saw from you back in auditions," Jasmine finally says.

"Derek gave me a few tips," I confess, nodding toward his work station.

Jasmine raises her eyebrows. "It's a welcome change to see camaraderie in this competition." Did she just give Nina a pointed look?

Jasmine moves on to Derek, and I can hear her fawning over his design. It's clear from the tone of her voice that she's impressed. As usual, his construction is spot on. I don't want to wish bad luck on anyone — especially someone who has been so nice to me — but would it be too much to ask for him to flub his stitching just once?

I keep working. I can't let myself get rattled by the competition. At this point, I know if could be anyone's game, so I need to be at my best. Only a few more stitches before I call it a night. Tomorrow, I need to work on tailoring the dress and creating the removable collar and peplum piece. And I still need to figure out how I'm going to incorporate the clunky chain Nina gave me, too. I'm determined to use it somehow.

I sew my last stitch and see Derek and Nina packing it up for the night too. From what I can see of their designs so far, they're determined to bring their "A" game to the final challenge as well. For the first time today, I notice the ache in my fingers and shoulders. The pain is a comforting reminder of all the hard work I put in.

* * *

The next morning Derek, Nina, and I are all back in the workroom bright and early. The camera lights seem brighter today, and my fingers feel much less capable.

I knew yesterday's Zen feeling was too good to be true, I think to myself.

Last night, it seemed like I had all the time in the world to finish up my final design, but today has been full of nothing but stitching mishaps. My thread keeps breaking, and my rushed fingers mess up even simple zigzag stitches. Oversleeping this morning didn't help either. Now, it's after eight at night, and I'm still trying to put the finishing touches on my dress.

Ignore the camera lights. I take a deep breath and slip the lining inside my dress, like I'm placing one tube inside another. I sew around the top edge of the neckline, then carry my dress over to the sewing machine to hem it. Once it's done, I slip it back on my dress form to keep it from getting wrinkled. I still need to attach Nina's chain necklace, which I've decided to use as a belt, but I don't want to do it while she's around, so I decide to focus on my removable pieces instead.

As the clock strikes ten, I grab the silk-cotton shirting to create my peplum ruffle. Sleep beckons, but I force myself to push the thought away. Why save anything for tomorrow? A cameraman yawns and trails after me, probably wishing I'd call it a night.

"Finishing up soon?" Missy asks. She looks almost as tired as I feel.

"Almost," I say.

"Good luck," Missy says. "And remember that no matter what happens, we're all proud of you."

I sit at my machine and think about what she just said. *No matter what happens? What does that mean? Is she trying to let me down easy already? Does she think those words lessen the blow of losing? Let's face it, at this point in the competition, no one is going to be happy coming in second.*

Trying to put Missy's words out of my mind, I get to work on the peplum, measuring the waist of my dress form and calculating how large of an opening I'll need to cut in the fabric to make it fit. I fold the fabric in half twice, creating four layers, then cut the correct amount out of one corner to create an even loop of fabric.

I hold the fabric up against my dress to figure out how I want it to look. Then I cut out another long strip of white material. Laying it out, I pin it and use a fabric marker to trace along the edge of where I want it placed. Then I unpin it and cut the material out. I add a few small stitches down along the two ruffled areas of the front on the peplum to reinforce them, then place the long strip around the peplum, pin it, and sew it in place.

I hand sew a couple of hook-and-eye closures to the dress and peplum piece so that it can be easily removed, then take a step back to admire my work. It's one of my best designs yet — I just hope it's enough. I can already imagine myself walking the streets of New York in it, sitting in meetings with fashion executives, and discussing the latest designs.

I place the dress in a garment bag and hang it beside Nina's and Derek's bags. I have to resist the urge to peek and see what they've done. I know their designs are probably their best work too.

Thinking back on all the different challenges, it's almost impossible to tell who will win tomorrow. Nina and I have been pretty neck and neck throughout the competition, while Derek has been at the front of the pack since week one. I can only hope the judges will see how much I've improved and how much effort I put into my dress. With the internship so close, there's no room for mistakes.

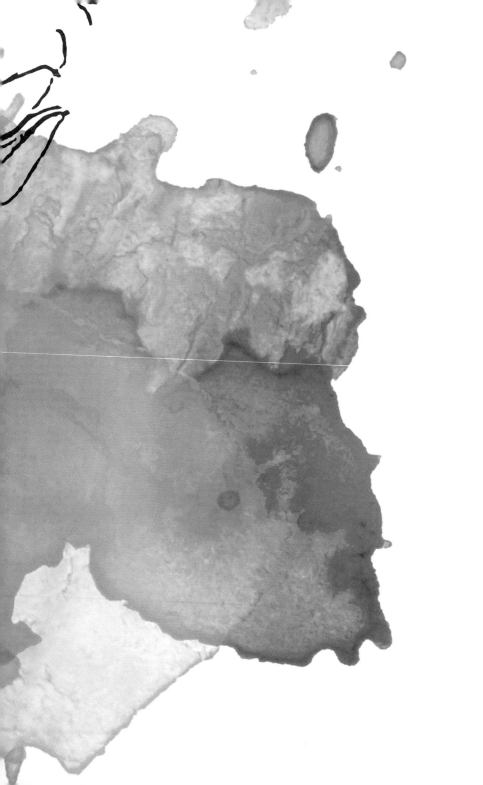

11

Monday is complete and total chaos as our family members are flown in from around the country, and producers work to set the stage for the big finale. Unlike earlier in the week, every seat in the room is filled with family members, friends, past contestants, and other viewers. Liesel is there — and so is her son, Jake. I haven't seen him since I visited Liesel's store for inspiration, but he's as cute as I remember.

"Break a needle," my dad tells me before he goes to find a seat in the audience beside my mom. Seeing him again has really made me realize how much I've missed him these past few weeks — even his corny jokes.

"That's not even a saying!" I reply with a laugh. "But thanks."

Liesel and Jake walk up to the stage, and Liesel gives me a hug. "I'm so proud to have been your mentor, Chloe," she says. "Knock them dead."

Jake gives me a hug too, and I blush. "You're going to kill it up there," he says.

Just then, a producer comes over and ushers me to the stage so we can get started. Nina and Derek are already there, standing beside their dress forms. The lights dim, and Missy, Jasmine and Hunter take the stage.

"Welcome, everyone, to the finale of *Teen Design Diva!*" Hunter says, and the audience cheers. "All the contestants have come so far. Let's watch their journeys."

A video montage starts up, chronicling clips of us throughout the series. The clips from the show are interwoven with interviews with our family, friends, and other people from back home. I shoot a surprised look at the audience. I didn't know they interviewed our family and friends.

I get to see Derek's house. His mom shows off his room, which is lined wall-to-wall with his designs. Apparently, he's one of six kids and captain of his school's swim and baseball teams. The producers interview his teammates about what a team player he is before moving on to a montage of his wins throughout the show.

Nina's video shows her gaggle of followers back in Santa Cruz. They're all giggling as they fawn over how wonderful Nina is. Then the video shows her house, where her mom talks about how helpful Nina is, finding time to help around the house when she's not busy designing.

Nina? Helpful? Huh. I never would have thought that to be true, I think. The video zooms through the challenges. First up is Nina's rodeo-inspired design during the final round of auditions, then the zoo competition, and finally the team challenge.

Then it's my turn. My video shows my parents and Alex talking about how much I love designing and how long I've been doing it. The producers show the outside of Mimi's Thrifty Threads, my favorite vintage store back home, and interview Mimi, the owner, who calls me talented and creative.

Then there's a brief video of me talking about my gramps and how he inspired me during the audition process. Watching myself choke up on screen makes my cheeks flush, but I watch proudly. My grandpa's inspiration helped put me on this show. There are also clips of me being named to the top fifteen, my toy store challenge win, and the Sony Wonder Lab.

When the video ends, Missy steps forward. "There's no doubt you'll be seeing all three of these talented designers for years to come," she says. "Just remember, you saw them here first!"

The crowd cheers, and Jasmine raises her hands in the air to ask for silence. "Tonight, however, is about choosing one winner. One of these designers will win the opportunity of a lifetime — an internship with a top designer here in New York and the chance to take the fashion world by storm. Let's get started."

The judges make their way to where Derek is standing and waiting patiently. "Can you talk us through your design?" Jasmine asks.

"I'd love to," Derek says with a charming smile. "I wanted something easy and effortless; I think everyone wants to look good at work without having to put too much thought into it. So I chose to create a shirt dress with a cropped blazer. Both pieces can work individually or be worn together as a complete outfit."

The judges examine Derek's shirt dress by itself for a moment, and then Derek adds the black blazer to the ensemble, transforming it into eveningwear. As with all of Derek's designs, the detials help set it apart — his blazer has minute, intricate additions like embroidery on the lapels.

Hunter nods. "I love the gold accents on both pieces," he says, looking as impressed by Derek as always. "The gold buttons on the shirt dress coordinate nicely with the embroidery on the blazer's lapels. I might be calling you for ideas sometime."

"Anytime," Derek says with a wink. "Happy to share."

The audience laughs as the judges move over to where Nina is waiting with her final design.

Even though I can't stand her at the moment, I have to admit Nina's design is stunning. She went for a vintage 1950s feel with a strapless, cinched-waist dress. Pink lace covers the fitted bust and a darker satin belt connects it to the flared-out black satin skirt.

"The dress is adorable!" Missy exclaims, echoing my thoughts. "But how would you make it office-appropriate?"

Nina smiles. "I'm glad you asked," she says. She slips the open-front black blazer she's been holding over her arm on to her dress form. "Adding a tailored jacket takes the dress from event-worthy to something that would fit in at any fashion internship," she says with a smile.

"Just lovely," says Missy. "Thank you."

I take a deep breath as the judges make their way toward me. "Last, but not least," Hunter says with a smile. "Chloe, tell us about your dress, please."

"I wanted to stick with my simple-chic style aesthetic," I say. "After all, that's what got me this far. So I decided to create a tailored shift dress in a monochromatic color palette. I used black rayon for the majority of the dress and a silk-cotton shirting for the collar. Metallic accents help add some shine to the ensemble and are a throwback to some of my earlier designs."

Missy comes closer and examines the chunky belt circling the natural waist of the dress — Nina's ugly necklace. I waited until just before the live show to add it. "This belt is really interesting," she says. "I love the contrast between the chunky chain and simple lines of the dress."

"That used to be a necklace," I tell her. "Nina kindly bought it for me."

Nina gasps.

"Very chic," Jasmine says. "But as well-tailored and elegant as this dress is, I'm not sure I see it being appropriate for an evening party."

"I'm glad you brought that up," I say, pulling out the peplum piece I created. I take the collar off the dress and slide the peplum piece around the waist. "These removable pieces make it easy to take the dress from day to night. With some metallic heels and cool jewelry, it will fit in at any evening event."

Jasmine nods. "Very impressive, Chloe," she says. "I love the modern addition of the peplum, and more than that, I love that you stayed true to your personal style. You've really created a cohesive collection throughout the course of this competition."

"Ladies and gentlemen," says Hunter, "I'm sure you're as blown away with these final designs as we are. But you'll have to wait until after the commercial break to find out which designer takes it all."

OTHER CONTESTANTS' *Designs*

DEREK'S INTERN LOOK
SHIRTDRESS WITH CROPPED BLAZER

NINA'S INTERN LOOK
1950S-INSPIRED DRESS
WITH BLAZER FOR DAY

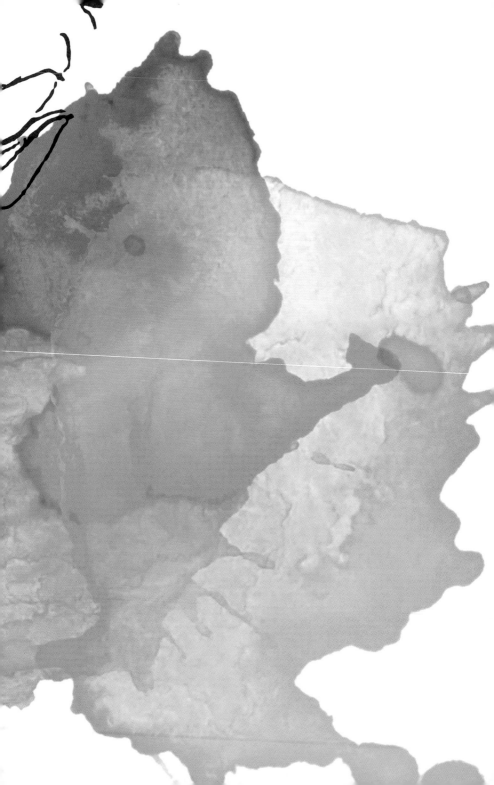

12

"Five, four, three, two, one!" the producer counts down.

Jasmine steps up to the microphone as soon as the commercial segment ends. "It's been a long road," she says. "And all three of our designers have grown throughout this competition. Let's give them one final round of applause."

The crowd claps and whistles. When they settle down, Jasmine continues. "We won't be criticizing anyone's design today because they are all fantastic. What it came down to for us was who took that extra step."

That could mean anything. Derek's shirt dress and jacket were so well made and detailed. And the judges have consistently loved his designs. As much as I hate to admit it, Nina's dress was adorable. I still like my dress the best, but that doesn't necessarily mean the judges did. It's still anyone's game.

"Who has consistently improved throughout the competition and grown as a designer," adds Hunter.

"The winner of the first season of *Teen Design Diva* and recipient of the fashion internship in New York City is . . ." Missy pauses. "Chloe Montgomery!"

Balloons fall from the ceiling and confetti rains down around me. I feel like I'm in a fog.

It's me, right?

They said my name?

I must not be imagining things, because my family, Jake, and Liesel are suddenly rushing to the stage. My mom and dad hug and swing me around.

"I knew you could do it, Chloe," my dad whispers.

"We're so proud of you, honey!" my mom exclaims, grinning at me.

Someone taps me on the shoulder, and I turn to see Derek standing there. "I'm starting to rethink helping you now," he says with a grin. "Kidding. You deserve it. Your design really was the best one."

"Thanks," I say, still in shock. "I can't believe it. Your stuff has always been amazing."

"Thanks," Derek says. "Well, congrats again. I'll see you around."

Derek heads off the stage, and I catch Nina's eye. "Good work," she says grudgingly before rushing off the stage too. Clearly she's not exactly thrilled for me. But I can't say that I blame her.

The judges hug me. "You've come so far, girl," says Jasmine. "I'm proud of you. And more importantly, I can't wait to see what's next for you."

A real compliment from Jasmine? I can hardly believe it. That's almost as good as winning the competition — and probably just as rare.

The world is spinning all around me. A cameraman shoves through the mayhem as Hunter hands me a microphone. "What are you feeling, Chloe? Did you have any idea you'd be here right now?"

"I'm feeling . . . shocked," I say. "This is unbelievable. To answer your second question, it took me a while to believe in myself, but I'm lucky to have supportive friends and family who always encourage me. I wouldn't be here without them."

I think of Mimi back home and remember my promise to mention her store if I won. Without her, there's a good chance I'd still be sitting in my room wondering if I should have entered the competition. "I owe a special thanks to a woman from back home — Mimi, who owns a store called Mimi's Thrifty Threads. She has been a huge inspiration. Look her up!"

Suddenly arms surround me from behind and I'm being picked up and swung through the air. When I'm back on solid ground, I turn around and see Jake standing there grinning at me.

"Congratulations!" he says. He leans in and gives me a kiss on the cheek. "Now that you'll be in New York, I'll get to see even more of you."

The balloons and confetti have stopped falling around me, but I still feel weightless. Through the window of the room, I see the bright lights of the city and the top of the Empire State Building.

"Chloe," Missy says, appearing at my elbow, "I hate to interrupt, but I need to steal you away for a bit. We need you to sign paperwork and meet your internship bosses. There will be a blog, Fashion Week prep, you name it. There's so much to do!"

Missy keeps talking, and I do my best to take it all in. I think about all the different versions of myself I've discovered along the way — Confident Chloe, Cowardly Chloe, Charismatic Chloe, Clumsy Chloe. I think of how far I've come.

Cameras flash in my face, but this time, I don't want to run away. I belong here. And I'll tackle everything that lies ahead on my own terms, as myself.

Just Chloe.

That's who I am, and it's enough.

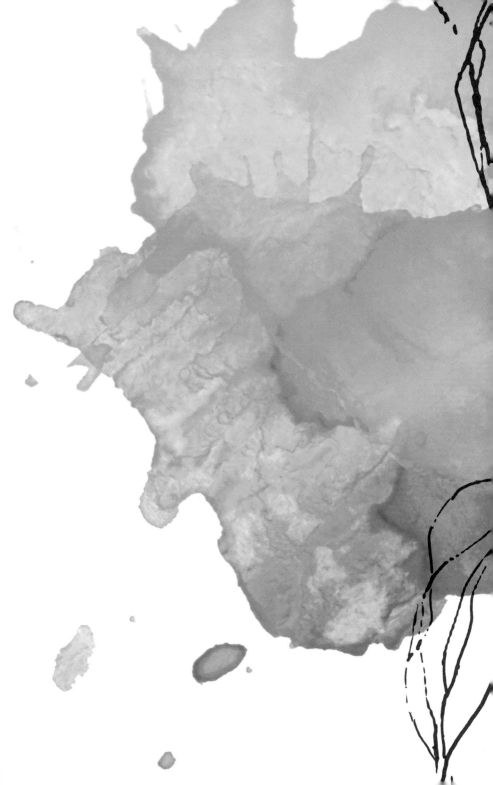

Author Bio

Margaret Gurevich has wanted to
be a writer since second grade. She has
written for many magazines and currently
writes young adult and middle grade
books. She loves hiking, cooking, reading,
watching too much television, and
spending time with her husband and son.

MARGIE

Illustrator Bio

Brooke Hagel is a fashion illustrator
based in New York City. While studying
fashion design at the Fashion Institute
of Technology, she began her career
as an intern, working in the wardrobe
department of *Sex and the City*, the design
studios of Cynthia Rowley, and the production
offices of *Saturday Night Live*. After graduating, Brooke began
designing and styling for Hearst Magazines, contributing to
Harper's Bazaar, *House Beautiful*, *Seventeen*, and *Esquire*. Brooke
is now a successful illustrator with clients including *Vogue*,
Teen Vogue, *InStyle*, Dior, Brian Atwood, Hugo Boss, Barbie,
Gap, and Neutrogena.

BROOKE